T0149448

The Perfect Kind of Imperfect

The Perfect Kind of Imperfect

Jackie Adams

iUniverse®

THE PERFECT KIND OF IMPERFECT

iUniverse books may be ordered through booksellers or by contacting:

iUniverse
1663 Liberty Drive
Bloomington, IN 47403
www.iuniverse.com
1-800-Authors (1-800-288-4677)

Because of the dynamic nature of the Internet, any web addresses or links contained in this book may have changed since publication and may no longer be valid. The views expressed in this work are solely those of the author and do not necessarily reflect the views of the publisher, and the publisher hereby disclaims any responsibility for them.

Any people depicted in stock imagery provided by Thinkstock are models, and such images are being used for illustrative purposes only. Certain stock imagery © Thinkstock.

ISBN: 978-1-5320-3225-7 (sc)
ISBN: 978-1-5320-3226-4 (e)

Library of Congress Control Number: 2017913837

Print information available on the last page.

iUniverse rev. date: 10/30/2018

A written gift for all generations who lost love ones and survived the news of all beginnings and changes.

A special thanks to my chief editor, Stephanie Zobrist.

I'd also like to thank my editors and proof readers at Iuniverse.

Another very special thanks to my cover photographer, Daniel Mandelker II.

Thank you to all who made this possible.

PREFACE

Did you not know how much I love you?!

Roger stands on the concrete porch in front of his stone cottage. Sure, he misses the home Harrietta and he once shared. Here, he is closer to her now, as she rests in peace. The best part is he didn't sell it to strangers. He made it their daughter's inheritance, from her mother, to share with his son-in-law and grandchildren. They're happy, and he is relieved strangers aren't making new, disconnecting memories within it. He stares across the street at Harrietta's tombstone tucked in tranquility underneath a blanket of nature.

The wind picks up. He smells snow in the air that hasn't quite arrived yet. He cradles his coffee mug in his hands. It's as warm as Harrietta's hands used to be. He'd come in after a long winter's day of construction, and Harrietta would always glove her hands over his. "Your fingers are so cold, Roger," she'd say with concern and love.

He'd smell fresh coffee continue its entrance in to the living room. He smiled and always replied the same comment over the years, "Cold hands, warm heart." This would lead to her arms wrapped around him in a tight hug that kept him as content then, as her memories do now. He quietly says out loud, "I miss you, Harrietta."

He turns, looking at his cottage once more, while wondering if this year he'll be strong enough to attend his daughter's Christmas dinner. Harrietta's only been gone for two years, but to the O'Dell family, every day without her feels like a decade.

On the opposite side of the cemetery is Margaret Stevens. For four years, every single morning, she has visited her Lexter. This year is no different for her, as she fixates on a piece of paper clinging to his name, inscribed on the tomb. She balances her weight against his gravestone, and grabs the rubbish off. She's busy thinking how rude others are to litter trash out of their passing vehicles, without a thought toward anyone else's feelings! And what do those caretakers do?! She will call them and complain as soon as she gets back home.

She traces Lexter's name inscribed on his stone. She whispers, "I miss you, Lex." Margaret straightens her body carefully, wadding the paper into her pocket as she begins making her way back to her home, across the street, toward the house they shared together for fifty-six years.

CHAPTER 1

Roger gets to his solid, red door he recently had the crew build after retiring from his management position at LDC Construction. Sure, the boys gave him hell, but Harrietta always wanted a red cedar door. She will, would have, he mentally corrects himself, loved this.

He sets his empty mug on the vacant telephone vanity that used to be Harrietta's favorite. She'd sit at it for hours talking to her friends, Sally and Velma. He'd hear one-sided conversations filled with laughter, gossip, and sarcasm. Antique shops, yard sales, and coffee morning plans to go out and about with her friends.

His daughter, Kathy, brought him a cellular phone last year for his 72nd birthday. He finds it senseless to use both a home phone and a cellular. He admits to himself burdening with the two is almost worth trading both for the one simple rotary he and his wife used to share.

Kathy said her husband, Arthur, took hours deciding the right gift. Personally, he calculates it as a financial waste, but he doesn't want to disappoint them. Kathy also told Roger not to be such a Flintstone lost in the Jetson era.

He had to smile, remembering his daughter, in her younger years, watching reruns of both. The

Flintstone's driving their stone-wheeled cars by the shuffle of their feet. And the drama of button-pushing a 4-course dinner from a machine in two seconds flat, in the duration of a Jetson's cartoon.

Roger hangs his coat on the wooden rack. He looks at his reflection in the circular hat mirror. He runs his fingers through his hair, turned white, and through his matching mustache and beard. With some weight he could easily be Santa Claus himself!

His doctor said he had the health of a middle-aged man. It's true his Harrietta always had him eat healthily. She would lecture how important self-care was. Even in the years his diet had slipped and dwindled while in mourning. He is still quite a handsome man.

Roger pours himself another mug of strong coffee. He sits at his table in front of the picture window overlooking the garden he started over the summer. It is now covered in autumn, withered leaves. The trees are hibernating until spring's wake.

He began his garden to bring a variety of fresh flowers to Harrietta every morning. During the fall, he brought her mums and sunflowers. Now that it's the start of winter, he walks with his faithful companion, Cassie, every night to leave Harrietta a letter.

Roger's wife brought Cassie home before she became more ill. She claimed she was a new breed titled teddy bear dogs. Roger had rolled his eyes and wondered how he was supposed to be seen with a damn teddy bear dog that looked as if it just arrived home from a pretty boutique.

He looks down at Cassie jumping up and putting her front paws on his lap. She has a tweed sweater matching her pink bows the groomer decided is cute. Too cutesy for Roger's taste. Cassie was supposed to remain small, being the runt. However, Cassie ended up as tall as a Great Dane, even surprising her vet. It made her a bit easier for Roger to bear in his brute, taught from his father's generation. Roger pats Cassie's head. "I guess we both miss her," he says.

CHAPTER 2

Margaret stares up at her two-story English Colonial. It is becoming too much for her to handle alone at her age of aches and pains, from the due process of time and years. She's often mistaken for her early sixties, even once thought to be fifty-eight! She remembered giggling like a school girl from the sweet advancement of a man, who could have been her son's age if she had one. Even as he boasted of his fifties, she knew he was merely a grown child, even if not her own. Still, the thought tickled her cheeks with a blush.

She's always amazed when she opens her door. The outside is manicured and pleasant enough, but nothing like the love and nurture Lex and she kept treasured inside their home. Their entry floor was a compromise of Lexter's love for white oak, which he inlaid himself, around her choice of Brazilian Redwood. They were amazed at how beautiful the colors and grains coincide together.

Margaret wanted Lex to feel as if every time he walked in he was inside his own resort. She'd pull his boots off him as he sat in his favorite recliner. Oh, these memories! What to do with myself? She felt tears well up in her eyes as she hung her coat in the entry closet.

She passes through the French doors to her library, generously full of books bought by Lex and her. Some were handed down by their grandparents, parents, aunts, and uncles.

The latest issue of Traveling Woman is sitting on her desk. She stands near it and realizes she's tired of trying to outrun the changes in her life. She's getting older with every year. Since losing Lex, she has seen more places than she had ever dreamed, or really felt discontent enough to feel she needed. It was more of an escape from the mourning she wasn't ready for.

Yes, she's had her bouts of crying on more than one occasion, many nights without her Lex next to her, some unbearable. A fit of tears, and she realized crying over it wasn't going to bring him back or change anything. So, she fled. She fled to Florida. She fled to Alaska. She fled to the Arizona Mountains. She fled to Paris. She even fled straight to all the musical shows at Branson, closer to her home. She went so far as to purchase a cozy lake front cabin, tucked away in a community far away from cities. A retreat. Margaret pushes away the magazine realizing she is home for the winter. Her summer cabin retreat is her travel now.

She looks for Grant's Cemetery phone number. She recollects she put it in a box, on the upper-shelf cabinet of the coat closet. She gets it down and puts her hand in her hanging coat pocket to retrieve the wad of trash.

She walks to her kitchen table in front of her patio doors, grabbing her cordless phone along the way. It's brighter here, so she sees well. She takes a seat. She is glad her blinds are open already. She doesn't have to fuss with them. She puts her phone down, turns its speaker on as it rings, and unfolds the paper. She reads,

My Harrietta,

Words can't express how much I think of you and miss you.

Before Margaret can finish reading it she hears, "Hello? Hello?!" The man's voice becomes disgruntled. "Hello?!" He says again impatiently.

Margaret opens her mouth to talk, but instead she quickly hangs up. She puts the phone down, pushes up on her glasses and brings the letter a little closer, reading from the top.

My Harrietta,

Words can't express how much I think of you and miss you. Every day a memory comes to visit, taking me by surprise. It's as if you've never left, except for the coldness when you're not near to me in thought. You know I've never been much of a romantic, but as I age I grow even more sentimental. Did I love you enough, Harrietta? I watch our daughter grow more and more. Well, you know, sometimes, when I'm watching her with Arthur, I wonder if I did enough, said enough. Seeing my grandchildren, the tough man inside me melts because I carry the softness and love that I watched you share with us. Why are you not with me! You belong here. Sometimes, I feel mad at you, but only because I can't hold you.

Margaret wipes away tears streaming from her eyes to her cheeks and chin. Maybe all her experiences missing Lex are typical. It doesn't feel like it when we are all living within our own lives.

She never attended groups for mourning. How could we all sit and listen to each other's misery! She traveled instead. No people patting her on the back, pretending to be empathetic toward what they couldn't understand. She could untangle from the unfairness of what she can't change.

She goes to her library and takes a folder from her file cabinet. She opens a manila one and puts the anonymous letter in it. She wonders, "Did I love Lex enough to make his years worth all the pain the cancer caused in the end?" Questions she never really thought about. Life was life, each day leading to the next, right?

CHAPTER 3

Roger stands at his kitchen sink finishing up the dinner dishes. He has a dishwasher, but hasn't quite figured it out. He's been living in his cottage for over a year. His pride is still intact after asking and being reliant on his daughter, Kathy, for every updated mechanical use.

Kathy is supposed to come over tomorrow and explain it to him, again. He doesn't have a problem with memory. He has a problem with everything that's supposed to be "easier" for us, feeling more complicated to him. It's overwhelming. He takes his dish towel from his shoulder and dries his hands.

Roger looks over to Cassie. "Are you ready?" He pats the top of her head and continues walking to his typewriter. He yanks the paper out, leaving the sound echoing throughout the living room. He always types on his hickory log writing table in front of the fireplace. It's warmer here and easier to express his feelings to her.

He folds the letter, creasing it in a three-fold vertical and slips it in the back pocket of his jeans. He searches the drawer one more time for a rubber band. He makes a mental note to remember to stop by the Smart Convenience Shop to buy more.

Yesterday evening, he noticed, the rubber band's elasticity snapped. He uses the rubber bands to keep the letters secure in the vase to the left side of the headstone. On the right side, he has it full of poinsettias.

He grabs Cassie's leash. She is eagerly wagging her tail in excitement. "Calm down, girl." He clips the leash to her collar.

He patiently waits for the more than usual evening traffic to clear. Since they started working on the 4-way of Kingston, his street has the repercussion of others conveniences. Cassie pulls forward with a tug.

Roger's shoulders slump as he nears, looking over Harrietta's dirt-covered, leaf-piled patches. Some grass grew. Some stolen by rain, creating small puddles of sunken mud in its place.

There are times he had to overcome that's taken everything inside himself not to dig deeper, open the damn casket and grab her in his arms. In his eyes, he saw her as whole, undamaged, with an angelic glow. Anything less would not be accepted or tolerated. The reality of what happens to a body was detached from Roger's senses.

He puts the letter in her vase. As Cassie sniffs around, she starts trying to dig her paws through, shuffling the remains of others artificial flowers that have blown over and the leaves Roger doesn't remove, hoping it keeps the ground warmer. "No Cassie. We can't."

He slowly maneuvers down to the wooden bench he made himself. He pulls Cassie in for a hug. They both sit there quietly, calmly, and stare at the headstone. There's a picture there of his Harrietta on it. She loved this photo. It was taken during their 50th anniversary. She didn't know the photographer they hired for the celebration had taken this picture until much later. She discovered it going through his finals and choosing which to keep. You can't see Roger in the photograph, but she was gazing at him with a huge, warm smile on her face. The photo captured truths of sincerity, loyalty, and love. It's more real than a camera can normally demonstrate, which is why Roger had chosen it.

Big snowflakes start to fall. Cassie is jumping up, trying to catch them in her mouth and falling right down with them. That must be where they get the old saying, "Raining cats and dogs". Roger's eyes amused within his thoughts. Cassie's size, falling amongst the snow was enough to pull him through as they make their way back home. He even laughed out loud! Shaking his head at his own immaturity.

Roger starts his fire with easy lit logs. He's too old to be out chopping wood, and he's smack dab in a city disguised as country scenery. He's keeping the few trees he has and even hopes to plant a dogwood in the spring.

Harrietta always admired the dogwood's petals on the ground, as it took off its seasonal changes. She'd playfully walk through the petals at the park, over the lush grass and then have the audacity to throw a few at Roger lightheartedly. Their laughter echoes in his mind, as he lights the fire.

CHAPTER 4

The next morning, Margaret begins her routine. She starts off with a pot of coffee, to help her with her morning walk to visit with Lexter. She has a bagel with blueberry crème cheese. Afterward, she has a glass of water with her multi-vitamins.

She walks over to her grand piano. The windows are hugging around it, framing the outside snowflakes that fall onto her pines. She is inspired with overwhelming thoughts she will humble herself within after her visit. If Lexter was still alive, he'd be standing there staring out! She'd play him a tune she'd been practicing.

She locks up her house and walks to the cemetery. She goes two sections over and one row back. As she is walking, she notices a piece of paper another section over. She wonders if it's to Harrietta or maybe this time it really is just litter. She would be going out of her way to retrieve it. She looks around. Nobody is here now. She questions herself, is it wrong?

Margaret excuses herself all the way to the piece of paper. She opens it, and sure enough,

"My dearest Harrietta,"

> It is between creases and black ink blotches. He must have typed it recently.

She wipes away the smudge it left on her thumb from holding it.

She puts it in her beige pants pocket, and makes her way back to Lex. She sets her book bag down, puts the letter inside the small pocket in the front of it and pulls out her throw cover she brought. She gets in her bag and pulls out her latest romance novel, "**Noel, the Christmas Angel who came like a snowflake.**" Sounds gaudy enough, but she couldn't help but to be curious of the story it held inside. She reads to chapter 5, puts her book down and looks up at Lex.

Margaret keeps hearing a dog bark, and it's really starting to annoy her. She stands up, slowly turning around, trying to figure out what direction the loud mutt is coming from. Everything gets quiet. She puts her things back in her bag and makes her way back home.

She must admit to herself, she made it home faster than usual. She is so intrigued with what is left to be said. Did he not explain it all in the last letter? What else could he possibly think of to say to a decaying body that cannot hear?! Doesn't she talk to Lexter, though? She's just as guilty.

She quickly makes herself some tea and sits at her kitchen table.

My Dearest Harrietta,

Where are you now? What is it you see? Are you floating in a spirit world? Or are you resting right near me? Are you in heaven?

I miss our talks. If I could take back even one day and hear you talk to me again, but I guess I do, don't I, living in all these memories of everything we shared together. Our daughter moving into our home has helped me somewhat. Still, everything we had comes with our laughter, our fusses, our memories. I'm not trying to let go. I'm just trying to somewhat exist. I'm both clinging to realizing you really are gone, while also gripping onto the thoughts keeping you close to me.

It's very confusing at this point, but I suppose there are lessons in it. Isn't this what we go through in life? Did you not know you're supposed to still be in mine?

Margaret adds his letter to the manila folder and shuts the file cabinet drawer. She shuffles around the room, slowly making her way to the grand piano. It hasn't been touched in over three years, beyond having her maid clean it. She had cried too many lonely nights playing her heart out. She shakes off the sad, lingering memories of those nights.

She sits and traces her fingers slowly over the keys. She notices some of them are loose now. She decides to call Steve, to have him repair them soon and tune it.

CHAPTER 5

Roger sits in front of his Remington typewriter. He rubs his hands together and squeezes his fingers inside each other. His knuckles snap, crackle, and pop. He thinks of his grandkids rice crispy cereal and smiles. He stares at the fire and begins finger tapping his keys.

Harrietta,

Christmas Eve is approaching too soon! This year, Kathy said I'm coming to dinner and she'll accept no excuses. I admit, she's right. It hurts to be close and not see you. Does this go away? What if I cry in front of the children and grandkids? I'm a grown man for God's sake. What if the grandchildren see me like that? I'm not ready, Harrietta. I'm not ready.

I don't want to disappoint Kathy and Arthur. I keep thinking of new gestures to get myself out of it. I guess there isn't one that's good enough.

Can you send me some thoughts?! A sign? Any sign that doesn't read, "a no way out", sign?

Lately, Cassie isn't the same either. I guess she realizes you're not coming here to live with us. She used to look out the window for days, just waiting.

I'd like to take her home, I mean, to Kathy's house with me. I know she'll run straight to our bedroom searching for you, only to realize you're not there either. Maybe she knows you're buried where we visit? Oh, I don't know, since when did I start trying to think for a dog? I miss you, Harrietta.

Roger stretches his arms and then stands to stretch his legs. He hears his cellular vibrating, and he tries to think of where he last put it. Cassie begins to bark. "Shhh Cassie, I'm looking for the phone." Cassie continues to bark, adding to the knock at the front door.

Roger peers out the window. He sees Kathy and Arthur. He opens the door. "You don't have to knock."

"Dad, I never know what I might walk into." Kathy smiles, wiggling her eyebrows up and down.

Arthur pinches Kathy's side playfully, "Stop making your father blush."

"Me blush? I'm too old for that nonsense. Where are my grandbabies?" Roger looks out the door one last time before closing it.

Kathy explains, as she straightens her father's collection of photography displayed on the wall. "They're at Velma's house. Velma's daughter, Tracy, has been staying the week to help Velma prepare for their Christmas Eve dinner. Velma's grandchildren came along this time, and she thought they'd enjoy playing with our kids. It was a last-minute decision. You didn't answer, dad, and after Velma called it worked out anyway." She continues, "The kids called wanting to stay overnight. We were reluctant at first, but Velma took the phone from them and talked us into it."

Roger asks, "A few minutes ago? I thought I heard my phone buzz. Geez, even superman isn't that fast." He starts looking around, searching for his phone again.

"No, dad, we called a few hours earlier, silly." Kathy picks up his cell off the breakfast counter. "Looking for this?" She dangles it in the air playfully with a huge smile of mischief on her face.

Roger smiles and replies, "My girl. What would I do without you?"

Arthur chides in, "I could think of a few things,"

Kathy's eyebrows become scuffled with aggravation, "Be nice."

"What's your problem, Arthur?" Roger asks, as he hands him a mug of fresh brew. "Let me guess, a morning without coffee?"

Kathy interrupts, "No, dad. I wish it was that easy to fix. The kids were sick over the weekend. Arthur had a casino trip planned with the guys. Mind you, the first one all year. I had to work, and our babysitter had school. Arthur said he didn't mind staying home, but failed to mention he'd be crabby afterward. I've been putting up with his attitude ever since."

Arthur takes a sip of his coffee and then responds, "Oh, come on Kathy. You'd be off too if the guys were calling you, bragging about what a great trip it ended up being."

Arthur stands up, "Do you have any crèmes, Rog?"

Roger points towards the counter, "Kitchen, by the coffee pot." He crosses his socked foot over his other adding, "Check the expiration date. It," Roger hesitates, "It came with me in the move." Roger thought about how it was Harrietta's. She always had two spoons full of crèmes with her four of sugar.

As Arthur walks into the kitchen, her dad looks her in the eyes. "Kathy, you really should be more understanding. Arthur loves you, and he puts you and the kids above all else. You should respect that in a man even if he gets moody afterward!" Roger sits on the couch and pats the spot next to him.

Kathy sits down next to him. "I know dad. It just gets old after the third time hearing him whine about it. How long will he use it as leverage? Today, he wanted me to make breakfast, AGAIN!"

"Breakfast," Roger draws his dramatic tone out, "Ooh no, worst problem, in the world." Roger and Kathy laugh together.

Arthur brings Kathy in a cup of coffee, "Here babe."

Kathy's smile gets even bigger, "Thanks."

Arthur takes a seat on the recliner clear across the room by the fireplace. Roger peers at him in concern, "Why are you sitting way over there, Arthur?"

"Kathy didn't tell you yet?" Arthur looks over at Kathy.

Roger slips on his Stetson, western boot. He asks, "Tell me what?"

"I.. I invited.. do you remember Angela?" She asks her dad.

"The little brunette with freckles?" He asks, grabbing a graham cracker from the coffee table and dipping it into his coffee.

"Yes," she quickly adds as fast as she possibly can, "I invited Shirley."

Arthur adds, "Shirley is Angela's mother." Arthur emphasizes the word *mother*.

Kathy grabs a couch pillow and throws it at Arthur. "You can be such a spoiled brat."

Arthur puts the pillow on the side of his recliner, picks his mug off the fireplace step, and replies, "Maybe I'm a spoiler, but I'm not a con artist."

Kathy lets out a huge sigh. "Dad, I didn't do it intentionally, like Arthur over there is suggesting." She gives Arthur an evil glare. She then continues to explain to her father, "Angela is out of town, and Shirley lost her husband quite a few years back. Normally Angela is home, but this year she had to travel north to see her brother's twins. Shirley couldn't go with her this year."

Roger asks, "Why not?"

Kathy answers, "I don't really know dad. I assumed it must be her health, so I invited her to our dinner." Kathy picks at a loose thread from her skirt.

"This better not be a sad attempt to set me up, Kathy Jane!" Roger watches Kathy look up with the same puppy dog eyes she always used when he titled her first and middle name. "I just lost your mother recently. I'm not ready for that. I'm not sure I ever will be." Roger says looking toward his sheep rug.

"Dad, I'm not setting you up. I'm being totally honest about Angela's call." Kathy stands and collects their empty mugs. She is taking them in the kitchen.

Roger looks over to Arthur and asks him, "Is this true?"

"I'm afraid it is, as much as I'd like to see you sand blast her." Arthur says standing and stretching his arms out long. "This place sure is cozy. I'm pretty sure I could fall asleep in seconds."

"It's a good thing it's time to go then, Arthur." Roger

smiles at him, and Kathy re-enters the room, grabbing their jackets from the coat rack.

"Your father is trying to get rid of me, babe." Arthur says, smiling at Kathy.

"Hasn't worked for me yet, dad." Kathy grabs Arthur's coat and passes it to him, before putting on her own. "We have to get going. I still have so much to do before we can leave the house. We will see you this weekend! No getting out of it." Kathy kisses Roger on the cheek and gives him a hug.

Roger opens the door. Arthur reaches out his hand for a handshake, and Roger says, "What, you want your hand kissed, princess?"

Arthur laughs. They hug and give each other a quick pat on the back. "See you this weekend," Roger says, while watching them walk to their oversized white SUV. Roger always teases, telling them they look more like an FBI squad than a family.

Roger decides to visit with his Harrietta this morning, instead of in the afternoon. He feels stressed, and he's not sure what to think about this whole Shirley business. He makes a quick phone call first.

"Where the hell have you been, buddy? I told you not to turn into a stranger," boasts Frank. Frank and Roger have been best friends since grade school. It's true, he did slack-off going for a drink with the guys and doing things after work once Harrietta became sick. When he lost her, he lost most everyone around him.

Roger runs his finger through his beard, "Hey, old buddy. My daughter has invited this woman to a Christmas Eve dinner. I'm trying to think of 1 out of 100 excuses to get me out of it. Have any advice?"

"Are you kidding me? Mary Ellen invited her sister. It can't be worse than that Rog! Maybe we should run to the bar first, get drunk, and somehow hope it'll fix it all."

"Frank, you're a genius! What time, and at Herb's Place?" Herb's Place was their hangout since first sneaking in with fake ID's at 19. They were caught, turned in to their parents, and lectured enough not to try it again.

"See you there at 11," Frank says. "Alright," Roger says, as he hangs up the phone and walks over to the cemetery with Cassie.

CHAPTER 6

Margaret is visiting with her Lexter. She's made it to Chapter 8 before admitting she's absolutely bored with her book compared to reading Harrietta's letters. She finally closes it and pulls out her memo pad for a list of things she needs from the store.

She jots down to call her nephew, Craig. Earlier, she had seen a fresh bouquet of flowers from him. I guess he's feeling stronger than he had during the funeral. It was her first time noting his visit to the cemetery. Is he still her nephew? How come he didn't come by the house?

Every time Lexter's brother, Holinder and his family, would come to Lexter and Margaret's home for the holidays, Lexter would rush to the door to greet his nephew, Craig. Before Craig aged, Craig would come running at a fast pace and jump into his arms excitedly yelling, "UNCLE LEX!"

They had a bond between them like no other. Of course, Craig grew into a teen and started finding a life of his own. He'd still make trips to see his Uncle Lex, to talk to him about things he didn't think his dad understood. Margaret gets up, looking down at the fresh, beautiful bouquet full of Poinsettia's.

She packs her blanket and memo pad into her bag. She begins to walk home when she hears a dog start barking. She turns around and walks toward its direction, through the cemetery.

Clear on the opposite side, as she starts to approach closer she sees a man visiting a grave site with a dog. Are dogs even allowed at the cemetery? It's not a zoo. What if he pees on the tombstones?

Margaret starts walking closer to the man and plans to give him a few thoughts. She stops when she is close enough to see him put a piece of paper in the vase. She notices it is vertically in a three-fold.

He walks off with the over-sized poodle or gold retriever. Maybe it's a mix of lab? When did dogs get so tall? And is this the Harrietta? She waits to see if the man gets in his car. She notices he walks his dog across the street and enters in the stone home. She walks past, reading the tombs, as if looking for some other spot.

Harrietta A. O'Dell

Oh my, it even has her photograph under her name. These are definitely her letters.

She could take the note out of the vase. She's curious to see what it says. What has gotten into her lately! She is disappointed in herself for thinking of stealing a poor, dead woman's letter for crying out loud! She slowly begins her way back home, without taking Harrietta's note.

As soon as she gets in her house, she goes directly to her phone and dials. She hears his familiar tone answer, "Hello?"

She swallows back tears, missing him so much, finally hearing his voice, and says excitedly, "Craig?!"

"Yes, this is him," he answers in a non-interested tone.

"This is your Aunt Marge. I saw the darling bouquet you left your Uncle Lexter. How marvelous!"

Craig responds in a more burdened voice, "Thank you, Margaret."

Margaret speaks up, "I was wondering why you didn't stop by. Can you come to visit with me?"

Craig explains bleakly, "Sorry, we're all getting ready for our holiday trip. We are going to Grandmother Vincent's home in Virginia. We will not be back until after the New Year's holiday."

"Oh, okay," Margaret responds, feeling more like she's burdening him and with a sense of rejection.

"Bye Margaret," Craig says, sounding detached. He disconnects his side of the call before she can even properly say goodbye or have fun.

Margaret stays standing at her piano, feeling tears mound, in realization the bye exchanged was more honest than she cared to admit. They had moved on, and she should too. Soon Craig will go off to college, probably out of state, as he used to talk about. He's too young and lively to be stuck entertaining his Uncle's widow. She tells herself not to take the call personally. Maybe it's their way of healing.

She gets up, puts on her coat, and checks her bag for her list. She is quickly avoiding too much thought and adding more denial to them than she cares to tread on right now.

She takes a quick look in her full-length mirror. She's been working on her posture with her physical therapist that comes to her home once a week. She's also been doing her exercises every morning and every night. She sees it has paid off. She stands straight, quickly looks herself over and puts on her winter baby blue stocking cap with her matching scarf and gloves.

She opts to walk to the store, instead of driving her

Cadillac. She's decided she's going to trade it in soon. She needs something easy to step into that can make it up her summer retreat's hill without the tires letting everyone know she's there. They tend to spin, spitting gravel everywhere!

What was she thinking when she made her final payment and collected her keys to the cabin?! Margaret knew exactly what she was thinking when her real estate agent, Tom, opened the door to her summer retreat!

The oak door, with a painted hummingbird glass center window, opens directly to the living room sitting area. She instantly saw an open floor plan covered with interior log walls. The living room has a huge fire place insert, and the stones surrounding it went straight to the second-floor ceiling. Above the exposed brick wall kitchen is a loft covered with two walls of handmade built-in book shelves with carved and curved edgings. You could look straight down to the living room and front door. The only thing connecting above the living room is the hall that leads to a huge outside second story terrace. The terrace overlooks a huge lake. Tom said at night boat lights can be seen. Across the lake from her cabin are other homes which have windows that will reflect on the water. Tom said it's even more beautiful during different seasons. Margaret can't imagine it ever being more beautiful than she saw it during summer. Tom said wait until Autumn.

Margaret's thoughts are sidetracked as the wind blows her supply list from her bag. She picks up her pace a bit trying to catch it. She's almost to the list when it blows straight to the dog that is tied to a post. The very same dog she had seen earlier!

Albeit, the biggest dog she has ever seen or been close to. The dog is looking cute in pink hair bows, but she wasn't going to grab her list. She commands, "Give it to me girl!" She continues to plead with the beast. "Come on now. I need that."

Roger sees a woman speaking to his dog. He looks at the cashier, and the cashier looks out the window. They both laugh.

Roger walks out with a few bags in his hand, "Um, ma'am, is there something I can help you with?" Roger puts his bags down.

"This mutt of yours has my paper." She attempts to try and reach for it feeling braver in the man's presence.

"I wouldn't suggest you do that. Here, let me try." Roger reaches for the paper, and Cassie wags her tail, opening her mouth and letting him retrieve it. He smiles, handing the slobbery paper to Margaret.

Cassie starts barking, and she jumps on Margaret. Margaret falls straight to the ground, landing right on her toosh!

Roger, worried, quickly walks over to her and says, "Good grief! Are you okay? Do you need me to call an ambulance?"

Margaret asks, "Are you being sarcastic?" She glares angrily at him imposed by his dog. She adds, "Once you move Dogzilla I'm sure I will be fine."

Roger laughs, "Dogzilla. I like that one." He moves Cassie another post over. He then reaches his hand out to help Margaret up and says, "I'm sorry."

Margaret dusts her fanny off and straightens her shirt. Roger sees a cut on her hand. He says, "Please, come back with us, and let me clean this up for you. It's the least I can do. I feel really bad about Cassie jumping on you."

She recognized Roger as the man who had written Harrietta. She looks to her hand that is scraped and says, "It's not so bad. I can clean it up in their rest facilities."

"Then you must not have used their rest facilities yet." Roger adds with a smile, "They're a mess. If I don't help you I will feel guilt all day! I promise you, I'm not a weirdo." Roger points a half block down, "Can you see the stone cottage?"

"I.. I know where you live," she tells him.

"You're a stalker?" He asks amusingly with a glow in his blue eyes.

Margaret explains, "No. I picked up what I thought was trash. It happened to be a letter from you to your, I assume, belated wife?"

For the first time, Roger was quiet. The comment added a red tint to his cheeks. Margaret felt awkward for feeling more confident after catching him off guard this time. Roger picks up his bags. "Sorry, I was just here picking up rubber bands to help secure the letters in place. I..."

She says, "There's no reason you need to explain yourself to me. And yes, I guess my hand could use a bit of help before I do my shopping."

"Great, I bought coffee! How about a cup?" Roger clips the leash to Cassie's collar, and Margaret follows him back as they laugh about the whole experience she just had and about the letters she found.

CHAPTER 7

Roger comes up from the basement and places the leash on the telephone vanity. He takes his coat off to hang it on the coat rack and puts his cap on top. He reaches for hers. "I will take your coat and hat, ma'am."

He says, "I know it's an odd time to introduce myself. I'm Roger, Roger O'Dell." He smiles, putting her hat on a wooden peg.

"My name is Margaret Stevens. I live on the opposite side of the cemetery." She follows Roger to his kitchen. He pulls a travel medical kit out from his cabinet, above his stainless-steel refrigerator. He washes his hands, and Margaret takes a seat at his table.

He brings his kit over and opens it. He takes out a small bottle of wound wash, Neosporin, and a band aid. He opens a small package of wipes, wiping away some dry blood, and he sprays her cut. "Does this hurt?" He asks her.

"Don't be silly. We are making such a big fuss over something so small. I'm fine, really," she tells him. She takes the band aid, trying to angle it to cover the scrape, but the two ends stick together as she tries to shake it lose from her fingers.

"Here, let me help." Roger opens a bigger band aid. He takes her hand into his, and she reflexes, yanking it back. He looks down at her confused, "Do you want help or not?"

"Sorry, it's just…" She blushes.

He grabs her hand back and quickly puts the band aid on. "There, see not so bad, and now it's done. I'll brew us some coffee now."

He goes to his kitchen and fiddles with the mugs and kettle. "It's really kind of awkward knowing you read my letters to Harrietta, because they've been very personal. Were there many?" Roger asks, debating if he should stop writing to her, because he had wondered if it was childish to do in the first place.

Margaret says, "There were two. I found them quite interesting. I love to read when I visit Lexter. You made my new romance novel a complete bore. I'd catch myself wondering what you would write to her next. I feel awful about that. I lost my Lex four years ago. I guess I've turned into an old, nosy widow finding life and amusement in the hopes of finding another of your letters. Is that sad?" She laughs at revealing too much; even wondering if her thoughts in stealing a letter would be better suited desperate as a more adequate description.

Roger fills both mugs and says, "No, I guess if I found your letters I'd be intrigued, too. I lost Harrietta two years ago, and I think it's still sinking in that she's never coming back. It's like I keep expecting her to."

Margaret says, "I'm not sure the feeling ever goes away, Roger. Of course, I mostly traveled. It's my first time staying put this long. I may have delayed a lot of my feelings."

"Can I call you Marge?" He asks as he hands her the mug of coffee.

She's quiet. The only one who ever called her Marge

was Lex. Roger looks at her. She replies, "My late husband called me Marge."

"Will it bother you if I do, too?" Roger cups his coffee in his hand.

"No, I suppose not," Margaret replies.

"Surely others called you Marge as well?" Roger sets his mug on a coaster and slides another coaster towards Margaret.

She sets it on it and fiddles with the mug's handle. "After losing Roger, I mostly traveled. I haven't been home enough to really visit our friends," she pauses a moment and reiterates, "my friends."

She continues fidgeting with the mug handle. "The only time I hear my name is when the hotels would call affirming my reservations or during check-in"

Roger says, "I hadn't retired. I had no intention to. After losing Harrietta, I decided to take my retirement and focus on our daughter, Kathy. Her mother and she were closer than most. They were happy and did many things together. They were best friends more than they were mother and daughter. Harrietta had Kathy young. They used to dream up a gift shop, and we started the loan process on our house. Harrietta ended up sick more than usual. We found out she had cancer, so we stopped brain storming the business. Kathy lives in the house Harrietta and I used to share, and I moved here." He becomes quiet.

When Margaret doesn't say anything Roger continues, "Why am I telling you all of this? I'm sorry." Roger feels guilt for burdening her with all his sad details.

Margaret says, "You're fine." She adds, "Do you mind if I get another cup of coffee?" She starts to stand, when Roger brings over the pot. She situates back on his kitchen chair.

When he's finished pouring them more, he takes the

towel off his shoulder. He places it on the center of the tabletop and puts the pot on top of it, leaving it there.

She asks, "Did **your** dreams work out, Roger?"

He sits down and takes a deep breath to relax. He meets Margaret's eyes and says, "Yes, my dreams did. I hoped I'd be the first to..." his voice trails off.

She knows he was going to say die. She quickly interjects seeing him thinking about it, "Wow!" Margaret says, "Good to hear. Some never get to experience contentment or love their whole life."

"What about you, Marge? Were you happy?" Roger pulls his mug closer to him and takes a sip.

"I was," Margaret replies as Roger's phone vibrates and shakes on top of the breakfast counter.

He repeats, "Was?"

Roger smiles, "I'm getting a belt clip for my phone. I'm always looking for it these days."

Roger retrieves it, "Hello? Hello?" Roger waits a bit, "Hello?" He shakes his head, removing the phone from his ear and staring at the display screen with a confused look on his face. "Are you familiar with a cellular?" He holds it towards Margaret.

"I never had one, and I'm not sure if I ever want one." Margaret stands and stares at the display with him. "Looks like you missed the call. It states it right there." She points on it and the whole screen moves. "Wow. Did I move that?"

"I see your knowledge about this is as bad as my own." Roger hears laughs outside his door. "Do you hear that, Marge?"

Margaret nods yes.

Roger takes her hand and says, "Shhh, I have a feeling there are two youngins outside my door." They both go in closer to hear what's being said.

"You go first," says a little girl's voice. "I'm too pretty to scare grandpa."

Roger looks at Margaret, covering his mouth to keep his laughter silent.

Margaret then smiles at him as Roger turns back towards the door.

His granddaughter says, "Stop rolling your eyes at me, or I'm telling mom when she gets back."

A little boy's voice responds, "I'm scared of you every morning."

"That's it," replies his granddaughter, "I'm telling mom!"

"Ouch, don't pinch me!" The little boy comes running in holding his pinched, sore arm yelling in excitement, "Grandpa!!!"

Roger looks behind him to see Marge had found a chair at the table already. Roger looks outside and sees his daughter waving as she drives away. He closes the door and turns around.

Roger bends down on one knee where his granddaughter sits and she gives him a kiss on his cheek.

His grandson goes under his opposite arm giving him a kiss on his other cheek. He says, "Mom told me to give you this." He tugs out a folded paper.

Roger opens the square folded paper and reads,

Dad, did you lose track of your phone again? Sorry, I had to drop and run, you saw how disappointed Arthur was when he missed the casino with the boys. This is my way of making it up to him.

Velma had to go see her sister-in-law at the hospital, so I picked the kids up. You offered earlier. Here they are!

Thanks dad, we love you.

Roger looks towards Marge, who is already introducing herself.

"My name is Margaret," she says as she pushes the little girl's bangs out of her eyes and gently touches her nose with her pointy finger. "And who are you?"

The adorable blonde-haired girl with sky-blue eyes responds, "I'm Eloise. I'm six-years-old."

"Dad says she's six years of knows it all," the little red-headed boy responds, making both Roger and Marge laugh.

Roger's grandson says, "I'm Harry." He shows Margaret four fingers, "And I am four-years-old." He stands taller and proud, before running off to the shelves at the fireplace.

Marge responds, "Well, it's nice to meet you both, Eloise and Harry." Harry runs back as fast as he can get his small legs to travel, before he trips. Some of the pieces to the game he's carrying land around him.

"I told you to slow down Harry," his big sister says in a stern tone.

"You're not my mom." Harry gets up off the floor.

"If you're mean to me, I won't help you pick up the pieces," Eloise says, as she folds her arms in front of her chest.

"I don't need your help," Harry says, as he sticks his tongue out at her.

Roger fills his mug with more coffee. "Sorry about this. Kathy and her husband Arthur have a date night at a casino. The kids were at a friend's house that had a crisis."

Marge holds her hand up, "No need to explain. This is your home, Roger. I should be going."

Harry says, "But I hurried to get this game." He shows a hurt, pouty look with sweet, big brown eyes.

Eloise joins in, "Please stay and play. Grandpa never

wins. He could use your help. We can play teams! That way nobody loses alone."

Margaret asks, "He loses every single game?"

"Yes," Eloise answers matter-of-factly.

"Every single one we ever played," Harry adds in, as he puts the final piece in its box.

Roger fills Marge's cup and smiles. He says, "Don't let us guilt you."

"As long as I'm not intruding or over exceeding my welcome." Marge replies and takes a drink of her coffee.

"Actually, it's nice to have company," Roger states.

Harry tells with a sad expression. "Grandpa never has company."

His sister yells, "Stop that, Harry. You talk too much."

"What? I'm telling the truth," Harry says as he sets up the board game making sound effects to entertain himself as he does.

Eloise takes the spinner from Harry, "You're not putting it on right. I'll do it."

CHAPTER 8

"I've never seen someone lose a game that many times." Margaret puts the lid back on the game box. She takes a seat on the couch, across from where Roger is sitting, on the recliner holding his sleeping grandson.

Margaret says, "I was sure you intentionally did it, until I witnessed it for myself. I was wrong. Six games later, I'm convinced, you really do have bad luck," she laughs.

Roger smiles and says, "Only at Chutes and Ladders. I play a mean game of Go Fish and Uno."

Eloise grabs a book from the hickory shelf, "Will you read to me, Margaret? Pleeease?" She hands Margaret a Sleeping Beauty fairytale. Eloise takes Margaret's hand, and helps pull her off the sofa.

Margaret responds, "I'm not sure how good I am at reading these days. I haven't read to anyone since my nephew, Craig, was about your age."

"Stop pulling on her, Eloise. It's rude." Roger bluntly tells her, giving her a serious look.

"Ask your grandfather if it's okay first." Margaret says, stopping Eloise before she enters the hallway.

"Graaaaandpa?" She bats her big, blue eyes drawing out the charm. "Pleeeeeeease?"

"I guess it's not hurting anything," Roger says.

Eloise yanks on Marge's hand, leading her further down the hall to a huge bedroom suite. Marge notes the fireplace is two-sided, and warms this room as well as the living room. She notices the two twin beds, obviously set up for previous nights with their grandfather.

Roger carries Harry in, and puts him in the bed closest to the windows.

"Do you mind if I use your toiletry?" Margaret asks.

Roger gestures a comical grin at her term of bathroom. "Not at all," says Roger. He points to a door she thought to be a closet. "Straight through there."

Marge opens the door that is framed with pink painted boarder and colored inside it with baby blue.

She is amazed by what she sees. A double sink, double closet, full wall horizontal mirror, small electric or gas fireplace, and the toilet area covered by a partial wall that separates it from the Jacuzzi.

The Jacuzzi sits in front of a huge, curtained picture window. Marge takes in the view of the backyard garden as she winds the blinds shut.

She looks at the rubber duck, toy cars, and bubble bath. She smiles. She's never decorated for children, and this tickles an unknown part of her life.

One side of the sink has princess perfumes, Hello Kitty body sprays, and fruit flavored lip glosses. The other sink has a plastic toy razor, with Spider-Man shaving crème and hand wash. Obviously, Eloise has separated her things from her little brother's for their visits. Margaret uses Eloise's kitty hand wash and locates the hand towel with cute princess crowns.

Margaret smiles as she opens the door to see Eloise patiently waiting. She sits on the side of the bed and opens the book Eloise hands her. She reads, until the very end, when she looks up and sees Eloise has fallen asleep.

She has the strongest urge to kiss Eloise on her forehead, as she had, many times, Craig. Instead, she closes the book, puts it on the end table, and turns the lamp off. She whispers, "Goodnight, sweet Eloise."

Margaret notices all the family photographs covering the hallway walls. She doesn't stand gawking, feeling as if she's taking more interest than she should be.

She walks into the living room, and she can see Roger through the door leading in the kitchen. He's doing his dishes. She enters and asks, "Why do you do your dishes by hand? You have a dishwasher. Is it broken?" Margaret enters the room.

"No, I haven't figured it out. Kathy was supposed to help me, but with all that's going on, I forgot." Roger dries his hands.

Margaret looks over the KitchenAid dishwasher. She sees it is a basic unit and says, "Once you have used one, you understand the concept to all of them. Do you have powder, liquid, or tabs to put in it?"

"Yes, it came with some." Roger reaches over the fridge, and gets a sample pack out. "Do I have to use this exact type? I didn't see any that looked like it at the store."

"No. You can use any that seems to work best for yours. As you use it more often, you will get braver and try different types. You will eventually find one that you like. In the beginning, I started with powder Cascade. Then I went to liquid. Now I just use the packets."

Margaret opens the dishwasher, and Roger watches her. "First, see this opening?" Margaret asks.

Roger nods, bending down to take a closer look, and then stands straight again.

She continues, "Insert the liquid, powder, or packets

into this." She pours the liquid in its opening and closes it. "See these selections on your dishwasher? Like your phone, they are touch compatible. Push the selection which fits your dishes. Right now, I see they are already clean. Is it okay if we wash them again, just so you know how to use it?"

Roger nods yes, "I put some of them in there yesterday, because I didn't have time to hand dry them."

Margaret shows Roger all the selections. "Heavy wash is for built-up pans, pots, and tougher soils." She then explains, "I mostly use the normal wash cycle. Go ahead and select it."

Roger selects the normal wash.

Margaret continues, "Now you push down, where it says start."

She waits for Roger to push it. After, she says, "Now it counts down until you close the dishwasher. 5, 4... hurry shut it."

Roger shuts it and they laugh.

She says, "When it finishes, this red light will turn blue. You have different heat settings on it. You get to take your pick. You'll know which to use when, soon enough. You can't go wrong. Don't let it intimidate you."

"Me, intimidated? More like aggravated!" Roger scowls his eyebrows. "There had been so many changes, I guess my patience has worn thin. Maybe I'm tired of learning and want something familiar."

"I understand, four years of it, and I'm still adjusting. I haven't even moved." Margaret walks toward her coat. "Well, I should be going."

Roger says, "I wish I could walk you home. The kids are too young to be left alone. I could call and see when Kathy will be back, and you could wait?"

"No, no need to rush them on my account. I am fine,

and the walk home sounds good. It's not as if Cassie will tackle me, will she?"

Roger laughs, "No. In fact, I need to let her back up from the basement. I'm pretty sure she's mad. She didn't get to see the grandbabies. Hopefully, she doesn't go waking them by jumping on their beds, playing tug of war with their blankets, and giving their faces baths."

Roger helps Margaret with her coat. She says, "I had fun, and thanks for sharing your family with me. I don't have children, so it was nice to have experienced time with your grandbabies."

"I believe they enjoyed you even more," Roger responds.

During Margaret's walk home, she thought a lot about how nice it would have been if Lexter and her had children. He couldn't, and after she never thought twice about being a mother. She was content and happy. They had thought about adopting, but both were busy with their education and careers. They were happily in love and self-indulged with one another. They never thought about death or about time robbing one and leaving the other alone.

She gets home, she opens her door, realizing for the first time since losing Lexter how very lonely and cold their home is. It hadn't always been this way. They had loved each other so much they couldn't miss what they never had.

CHAPTER 9

"Grandpa! Grandpa! Wake up! It's morning already!" Eloise tells him. Harry starts tickling his bare feet, and Cassie isn't so innocent either, as she starts nipping at his toes.

Roger says with his raspy morning voice, "Okay, okay. You win!" He stretches. "You have to stop jumping on my bed, though. I'm too old to feel like I'm on a boat."

Harry takes a pillow in his hand and uses it as a shield toward his grandpa. "And I'm the pirate!"

Harry holds an arm out, pretending it's a sword and points it toward Eloise, "I have caught you! You must walk the plank!"

Eloise giggles and says, "Oh no! You can't keep me. My prince will save me!" She puts her hand on her forehead to add drama to their creativity.

"Stupid, there aren't any princesses in pirate stories." Harry rolls his eyes at his big sister. "You should know that!"

His grandpa stands, picking Harry up in his arms, "Don't call your sister stupid, or I'm going to hold YOU captive!"

"No no no, you can't!" Harry wiggles his arm loose grabbing a pillow and hits his grandpa with it.

Roger puts Harry back on the bed and picks up the other pillow. "Oh, yes I can!" He hits Harry with it.

"Mom always says, 'boys will be boys.'" Eloise becomes more sophisticated than the other two. "Come on, let's start breakfast, grandpa!"

"We have nothing here! How about we go eat at the diner?" Roger shuffles through his wardrobe, pulling out his jeans and a flannel. "Go change into the clothes your mother left here a few weeks ago," he instructs them. "I will call your mom."

The kids can be heard pitter pattering down the hallway as they race to see who can get dressed faster.

Eloise calls down the hall. "Can we walk grandpa?"

Roger grabs his loafers and heads toward his recliner in the living room. As he sits and slips one of his loafers, he responds, "Only if you promise to hold my hand. Harry, the same goes for you!"

Eloise and Harry both nod in agreement. "Can Cassie come too?" Harry asks, as Eloise ties his shoes.

"Not today, kiddos. Cassie had quite the adventure yesterday and is getting a pre-re-leashed reputation as Dogzilla!"

Harry repeats his grandfather, laughing, "Dog-zill-a."

Eloise starts laughing, causing Harry to laugh even more.

Roger makes the call to his daughter, "Hey Kat! I'm calling to let you know the kids and I are walking to the diner for breakfast."

"Okay, dad, Arthur and I will meet you there. Love you." Kathy hangs up before Roger can ask how their date night went.

Roger locks his door and each of his grandkids take a hand. "Good news, kids! Your mom and dad will be joining us for breakfast."

"Awww, I was hoping to stay longer. I want to play

more games with Margaret and you." Eloise stops on the sidewalk, causing a halt to Harry and Roger's next step.

Harry spews out, "Watch it, Eloise. I almost fell!"

Roger explains, "Margaret is not coming over today. You're more than welcome to stay and play board games with me if you want."

"It's funner with more people, though." Harry says. "You always lose."

"More fun, Harry, not funner." Eloise corrects her little brother.

"Maybe your parents would like to play a game with us?" Roger suggests they ask them.

Eloise says, "Mom will think we are bugging you. You have to ask her yourself, Grandpa."

They enter the diner. It is full of people! Roger tells Jack, the owner, he will wait until the next table for five opens. Meanwhile, he and the grandkids pick tall stools at the counter. Harry and Eloise spin their stools in circles, laughing at how dizzy they are becoming.

CHAPTER 10

Last night, Margaret was up later than usual. She kept replaying everything that happened to her. She also ended up sleeping later than usual, and she's still in bed. She's laughed more at herself last night and this morning than in all of Lexter's absence. She's also embarrassed, because she's STILL replaying everything that happened to her!

She laughs at herself again, deciding she refuses to think about him and his family anymore. She will go for breakfast. The house has never been so quiet and lonely. It will do her good to be around others.

She walks to her bathroom suite and studies herself in the mirror. Her color looks even better than usual. She has natural tints in her cheeks, and her eyes are full of bright green mystery. Her hair, most have to bleach to get as white as hers has become. She's no spring chicken, but she'll never stop believing she's beautiful. She says, "We are what we feel."

She walks to her wardrobe and decides on a pair of black pants, a peach turtle neck, and with her comfortable black slip-on loafers she will not have to bend a single time. Her physical therapist said the bending is fine. It gets her joints adjusted. Of course, she doesn't have the "help I've fallen button and can't get back up" a pocket push away.

She fell once before, and the hospital made a big deal of it. Ever since, she's been absolutely spoiled with therapists coming to her home and her visits to the doctor. A handsome doctor, too. One look at him gets all the ladies wishing they were thirty or forty years younger. She dabs on a bit of lipstick.

She puts her coat and scarf on. She grips her gloves out of her coat pocket, and she opens her front door. She hesitates a moment and turns back around. Everywhere she looks is a memory of Lexter. She finds herself in a trance for a second or two with her eyes left in the direction of the floor. She closes her door slowly and gently.

Margaret walks over to the Donut Hole across the street.

As soon as she enters, she hears, "MARGARET? It can't be!"

Margaret turns from the counter, and there is Sally, Sally Marshalls.

"It is you! Margaret Stevens! I thought you had moved! I never see you out in your garden anymore. I look over occasionally." Sally wraps her arms around Margaret.

"Sally! It has indeed been a long time! I haven't ate here since..."

Sally interrupts, "Since you lost Lex! I know. I'm still here, Margaret! It hasn't been the same around here either. We have all new waitresses and waiters." Sally guides Margaret to a table. She lowers her voice, "And the manager is a complete jerk."

"Fire him. You still own it, don't you, Sally?" Margaret asks in sudden realization things may have changed in her absence.

"Yes, I'm still the proud owner!" Sally smiles and says, "I can't fire him. I need him." She looks at Margaret again, "I sure have missed you!"

"I've missed you too, Sally! I was so busy traveling and staying away from here. I'm sorry I haven't been in. I wasn't being intentionally selfish."

"I assume you still drink coffee, black?" Sally sees Margaret nod and fills it to the rim.

"It's lonely at home," Margaret says aloud before she has time to think. She quickly adds, "I'm so glad I traveled."

"So, invite me!" Sally suggests.

"Invite you? Did I hear right?" Margaret looks up.

"Yes, invite me to your house, for coffee," Sally repeats louder. "I could use a friend. Andy and I broke up recently, and I haven't been too happy about going back to his apartment."

"What happened to your house?" Margaret asks.

"I'll tell you all about it! How about we get together after my shift? We can go grab a bite to eat for dinner or we can just drink coffee at your place."

"Let's meet at my house." Margaret replies. "Afterward, we can get something to eat. I would cook, but I had an incident with my shopping list that led me astray."

"That sounds either dangerous or exciting. I can't wait to find out. It's a deal." Sally looks at the oversized clock on the café's wall. "See you at 4pm." She takes her pen from her apron, "Now, what can I get you to eat, old lady?"

"Takes one to know one," Margaret says and laughs.

Margaret notices she has held her age well, too. Sally had started out as a teenage waitress in this café. She then invested in it and purchased it herself.

Margaret realizes how good it feels to be playful and

not so often stuck in the seriousness of pulling through each day. She is content, realizing coming back to Lex's and her favorite place for breakfast isn't as hard as she thought it might be.

CHAPTER 11

"Come ooon, mom. Grandpa already said he has nothing planned." Eloise layers her convincing tactics on thicker, "We never do anything as a family!"

"That isn't true. What about holidays and the plans we have this Christmas Eve?" Kathy asks her daughter.

"That's with everyone," Eloise says. She impatiently specifies, "I mean just us with grandpa."

"I have the day off. I don't mind playing Chutes and Ladders with the kids." Arthur says as he raises his finger in the air to get the waiter's attention. "On the other hand, watching your dad lose again could be a different story."

Roger slinks his shoulders, "I'm really getting a bad board game reputation."

Each of them laugh.

Kathy asks, "Are you sure you don't mind, dad?"

"I couldn't think of a better way to share my day. Besides, my reputation is on the line!" Roger puts his napkin on his lap, "Time to defeat and conquer." He raises his cup of coffee for the kids to cheers with him. "Tonight, I will win!"

"Grandpa, can I go first this time?" Harry asks, as he stacks a pile of sugar packets on top of one another, building a fort against the salt and pepper shakers.

"Youngest first," Roger responds, thinking about

how Margaret touched their nose tips as she spoke with them. Her gestures and grace with his grandkids adds spunk to his mood.

"Hi," says the waiter. He looks and sounds annoyed with his job. "My name is Don. I will be taking your order this morning." He stares at Kathy a bit too long, until Arthur coughs a bit too loud.

Their table is the noisiest in the diner and gets even louder as they start discussing amongst each other which orders they should or shouldn't pick and why.

After the last drink and food order were selected, Don walks off to retrieve their coffees and juices.

Roger asks, "How was your date night?"

Arthur mocks condescendingly, "Yes, Kathy, how WAS your date night?" He raises one eyebrow with a twinkle in his eyes.

Kathy replies, "Dinner was enjoyable. I was finally able to take my time chewing without the kids calling my name, or needing something in the process."

"I do not do that! You can blame yourself for adding another kid when you did perfect the first time," Eloise states.

"Boys rule, girls drool," Harry boasts.

The waiter brings their drink orders to the table, as each person passes it to its rightful owner.

Harry says, "Eloise's glass is bigger than mine. It's not fair! I'm a big kid, too!" Harry sits on his legs and feet, making himself taller.

"Sit right, Harry," Arthur says, as he puts his hand on Harry's shoulder. "You get the one with the spiral straw."

Eloise asks, "Can we call Margaret and invite her to play?"

Kathy and Arthur turn quickly, staring at Eloise. Kathy asks, "And who is Margaret?"

Roger was getting ready to explain when a lady approaches their table. "I thought that was you Kathy! Do you remember me?"

"Of course I do, Shirley. Angela was my best friend! Your house was my second home!" Kathy stands up and gives her a hug.

"Angela told me of your invite to Christmas Eve dinner. You are such a sweetheart, Katherine. Would you like me to bring a side dish or beverages? Maybe a dessert?" Shirley leans against Roger's chair.

"You can bring food if you like, but it isn't necessary. Definitely bring a beverage of your choice." Kathy sits back down. "Have you had breakfast yet?"

"Yes, I ate with Betty. She left moments ago. I should be going, too. We are going to a church lot sale this afternoon." Shirley says as she searches through her bag.

"Do you need help getting out?" Kathy stands again.

"No, dear, you sit right down, and enjoy your meal. I may be old, but I'm not senile." Shirley stands taller.

Roger laughs. "Watch how you talk to us older folks, Kat. Respect doesn't have the same quality when you're on the other side." He winks at Kathy.

"I'm sure you remember my dad, Shirley." Kathy angles her head toward her father.

Shirley moves closer to him and gets right in his face, getting a closer look. She says, "I can barely see these days," and gives him a wink.

Roger is sure he can feel his cheeks warming. Was she flirting or was she serious?

Shirley explains, "I have eye surgery next week. I will be blind as a bat for a few days, but my new glasses will do wonders! I may need some help then. Will you be available Kathy, when the time nears?"

"I'm working full-time, helping at the library, while

attending night classes. We had a retiree come in last week to help train our new staff. It's been chaos this past month." Kathy looks from Shirley, over to her dad, and gives him "the look", kicking his foot under the table.

Roger coughs up a... "I may be able to assist you, Shirley." Roger tears off a part of the receipt and puts his phone number on it. "Call me if you need me." He hands it to Shirley.

When Shirley puts the paper close to her eyes, she reads out loud to be sure she has it right. Roger feels relieved knowing she wasn't seducing him after all. He can't help but to smile at his own overly egotistical age. He verifies, "Yes, that's the right number, Shirley."

Harry says, "Can Shirley come to our game night?"

Shirley asks, "And these two must be your darling children, Kathy?"

Eloise interrupts, "No, Harry! She already told you she is going to a church lot sale." Eloise looks at Shirley and explains, "Brothers, they only hear sometimes!"

Kathy makes the introductions. "This is Harry and this is Eloise."

Shirley smiles and says, "You are both absolutely precious!"

Kathy grabs Arthur's hand, "And this is my husband, Arthur Taylor."

Shirley nods and smiles at Arthur. She responds, "Beautiful family."

Kathy points toward her dad, "Of course, you know my father."

Shirley says, "No, I never actually met him." She pushes up on her eye glasses and straightens her posture. "I've heard much about him through Harrietta and you, but he was always working."

Roger replies, "Roger, Roger O'Dell."

CHAPTER 12

Margaret and Sally are sitting at her kitchen table, sipping their coffees and discussing Andy. "I can't believe he treated you that way after all you've done for him over the years, Sally."

"I figured it would happen, Margaret. I was surprised it lasted as long as it did." Sally traces her cup's rim with her finger. She continues, "He was ten years younger than me. Hell, Margaret, even men my age date women barely through their twenties. I'm sixty-two years old. What was he going to do with an old woman like me! He's in his prime."

"You don't know old until you've reached my seventy-four. I thought you said he was fifty-two?! Hardly prime, Sally. Men in their primes are in their thirties and forties." Margaret stands to stretch her legs.

"Margaret Stevens, are you suggesting I date even younger?!"

"Not necessarily, though if men can, women can too." Margaret puts her hand over her heart, "My, my, what is this world coming to!"

Sally fiddles with a thick strand of hair that fell from her upswept bun. She tucks it back in and says, "There is someone I have been talking to over the past few months."

Margaret picks up their cups and carries them to

the sink. She looks over the frame of her glasses that have slid downward from her turning too fast. "Sally Marshall, you tell me this instant!"

Sally laughs again, "Jack Wright."

"The same Jack Wright that owns the diner in town?! I know him! Lex used to play cards with him and Marty, Hugh…" Margaret pauses and puts her finger on her bottom lip. "Oh, what was that other fellow's name? It's at the tip of my tongue."

"Is it Herb? Jack has a friend who is constantly at his diner.."

Margaret interrupts excitedly, "Yes Herb," she answers in relief.

Sally says, pleased with herself, "He's still around!"

"Does Jack know you're interested in him?" Margaret asks, as she turns the coffee pot off.

Sally answers, "He's flirted with me a few times, but usually before Andy arrived. I can't tell if Jack was just being overly sweet or felt non-threatened by the fact that I had a boyfriend? If he's building up my confidence after he overheard Andy treat me more like a burden? Or if he's like that with everyone?" Sally reaches over the table for the crème and sugar and takes it back to the kitchen counter.

"My goodness, Sally, no confidence in yourself, and not much faith in the male gender either." Margaret says as she walks to her coat closet.

Sally responds, "I guess you're right," following behind Margaret.

"Speaking of, do you want to eat at Jack's place?" Margaret asks, handing Sally her coat and gloves.

Sally responds, "Sure, sounds good to me."

CHAPTER 13

"Well, well!! Miss me already, Sally Marshall?" Jack asks, taking the menus from Don, his employee.

Jack says to Don, "Your work day is over. See you tomorrow morning at 6am."

Jack seats Sally and Margaret to a nice table with the best view of his pine and cedar trees. "And what would you beautiful ladies like to drink?"

"I will take a tall glass of iced non-sweet tea, please," Margaret says, as she looks over the menu.

"Of course, Margaret, it sure has been a long time since I've seen you!" Jack smiles warmly at her.

She responds, "Lots of healing, Jack, lots of travel." Margaret repositions her silverware.

Jack looks toward Sally, "And what would you like?"

Margaret slyly looks up from her menu, studying Jack as he waits for Sally to respond. She notes definite interest and attraction from Jack with his change of facial expressions, eyes, and body language, as he stands even closer to Sally with each waiting moment.

Sally looks up and requests, "I will take your famous mug of hot cocoa, Jack's Style."

"Sure thing, Sally." He starts to walk toward the counter and stops suddenly, like he wanted to say something, but changed his mind.

Margaret waits until Jack is out of ear shot. She

says, "I noticed he definitely favors you, Sally. Maybe you should mention your breakup with Andy?"

Sally anchors her elbow on the table with her chin resting in her hand palm. She asks, "You don't think I'm moving too fast?"

"Honey, we aren't getting any younger. You are a beautiful, single woman. You are successful, not to forget to mention, you and Jack have a lot in common."

Jack walks back and sets their drinks down. He then slips a paper out of his back pocket. He hands it to Sally. She looks it over as he asks, "Do you ladies have time to help me decorate the diner for it?"

Sally answers, "I do in the afternoons," and hands the flier over to Margaret.

Margaret reads out loud, "New Year's Eve Diner Dance."

Sally says, "I can pick you up on my way there, Margaret."

"Okay, Sally." Margaret smiles in agreement.

"Sign me up, Jack. I've been busy being trained at the library by the most patient young lady, Kathy, to check books in and out as a sub when our librarian is sick or when they get too busy. It doesn't occupy my afternoons, though." Margaret explains.

"Kathy, Kathy Taylor?" Jack asks.

"Yes," Margaret responds.

Jack says, "She was just in earlier with her father and her husband."

Margaret says, "I'm not sure how much I can help with the decorations. It's not as if I can reach high or hang anything."

"Kathy's dad is a handyman. He's bringing his tools and ladder." Jack rolls his eyes. "He complains my ladder is falling apart."

Sally blows the steam away and adds a few pieces

of ice from her water, to her mug. She asks, "When would you like us to start?"

"Tomorrow," Jack asks.

Margaret looks around his diner, "Jack, decorating in here won't take that long if you have the men move the tables and chairs?"

"I," he hesitates, "have opened up the back area I usually use for storage." Jack holds up a hand, "Now before you change your minds, it has already been cleared out and cleaned. The foods and desserts will be in here on buffets. This way they can still use the tables. It's still dark and bleak in the area we'll be using for a band and dancing. I need ideas on where to put the decorations that are already ordered."

Sally suggests, "How about we come tomorrow?" She looks at her watch, "About the same time?"

Jack smiles very big and feels relieved. "6pm it is!"

"Margaret?" Sally asks, waiting for her approval.

"Sounds like an exciting challenge to me," Margaret agrees.

CHAPTER 14

"Grandpa, I thought you said you were going to win this time?" Eloise says as she continues putting the board away.

"I'm practicing for the big win." Roger says as he kisses the top of her blonde head.

Harry suggests, "Maybe we should try a new game, Grandpa?"

"Maybe grandson," Roger says as he shuffles Harry's red hair.

"Arthur, can you help me get to the ladder in the shed?"

"Sure, Roger. Need a light bulb changed?" Arthur asks.

"No, I can reach my lights with my step ladder. I'm helping Jack prep for his New Year's Eve party at the diner. Do Kathy and you want to go? I can reserve a table for you," Roger says as they walk out back.

"We decided this year we will relax at home with the kids. We'll rent some movies, make popcorn, and watch the parade on television. Eloise is excited for us all to count down for the ball drop. Harry is going to try to stay up all night, even longer than Eloise. It's a competition between them." Arthur smiles and ruffles through the boxes, pushing them to the side. "Are you going, Rog?"

"I don't know, probably not. I'm getting too old to go to proms for adults," Roger adds, "Besides, I haven't danced in years."

Arthur says, "It would do you good to get out and mingle. You won first place at the Moose Lodge dance competition,"

"That was over a decade ago, Arthur, and need I remind you, I had the best partner." Roger says, as they pull the ladder out and walk it around to the front.

Arthur helps Roger set it in the back of his truck. "I know it has been hard. You took care of Harrietta for two long years, and then losing her. I can't say I understand how much that must have hurt, Roger. But you have to live! You need to have fun and be in the moment. Harrietta would want that for you, Rog. She'd be mad at you sitting around sulking, and using her as your excuse to do it."

Roger says defensively, "I'm not sulking, Arthur."

"Yes, you are, and you have been." Arthur gives Roger a pat on his shoulder.

Roger looks over at Harrietta's grave and turns to look at his stone home. "Maybe," he says more to himself than to Arthur.

CHAPTER 15

Margaret hears Sally's horn. She quickly takes her keys out of her purse and locks her door.

Sally says out of her jeep's window, "Well, you sure look pretty!"

"These old jeans, these were the work clothes I wore when working on the house with my Lex. They sure bring back a lot of memories." Margaret gets in slowly, as she does, she's thinking of all her times working together with Lex.

She was not surprised to still fit into her jeans. Losing him, lost her the weight she had gained trying to cook foods to entice him to eat. She gained weight as he grew to skin and bones with each passing day, and she lost him more and more each passing night.

Sally saw this look before. She knows Margaret is still thinking of Lex. "I hope I look as good as you do in jeans when I'm seventy! And look at you climbing into this jeep like it's nothing. Sorry, it's so high up." Sally puts her jeep in reverse.

"Seventy-four," Margaret corrects Sally and grins. "I admit my physical therapist has been keeping me in tip-top shape since arriving home. She demands she does her worth," Margaret says with confidence. "I work hard three times a week busting my bottom," she admits. It feels good to have others notice at her age.

She deserves to feel good about herself. It feels better than feeling bad about not having her Lex.

When the ladies enter the storage area of the diner, they see five men working. The first man is setting up a stage, the second man hanging a disco light, the third man working in the restroom painting, and the fourth, Margaret recognizes, is talking to Jack.

Margaret asks, "Jack, did you decide to have your party early?"

Jack responds, "Not without you ladies!"

Margaret looks to Roger, "Good to see you again," she says to him.

"You two know each other?" Sally asks, confused. "I was just getting ready to introduce you."

Roger replies, "Yes, she had the pleasure of getting a knock-down hug from, who she describes, Dogzilla." Roger smiles at Margaret as the others laugh.

Marty walks over and hugs Margaret. "I haven't seen you since Lexter's funeral."

Jack stands close enough to Sally that she gets very quiet, not even saying a word. Margaret felt tickled by her unusual non-talkative self.

Margaret gives Marty a hug back. "Good to see you, too, Marty. How is Louise doing?"

Marty answers, "She's doing fine! I'll bring her by! She'd love to see you again."

"Sounds great, maybe you can bring her here at 6 o'clock tomorrow evening, and she can help us?"

"It is a sure bet, Marge," Marty replies.

Margaret smiles and says, "A sure bet would be placing one against Roger's game losses."

Right after, Roger and Margaret look at each other and laugh out loud.

Jack asks, "What's so funny?"

"Just something personal, is all," Roger replies.

Jack wiggles his eyebrows up and down, "Oh? Personal you say?"

Roger quickly repositions his ladder.

Jack guides Sally and Margaret toward the two tables full of boxes. "This is the stuff, ladies. It was delivered yesterday." Jack walks back to join the guys.

Margaret looks at Sally and asks, "Stuff?"

Sally and her start opening the boxes to look inside. As if on cue, they both repeat Jack, after seeing all the things and say simultaneously, "stuff." They laugh at each other sharing the same thoughts.

Margaret adds, "Lots of stuff."

Sally says, "Roger keeps looking over at you, Margaret."

"Oh, don't be silly. He's just curious about me." Margaret doesn't dare look, and she feels her cheeks go warm.

Sally says, "Roger was my best friend's husband. They were so in love. Roger had such a hard time watching Harrietta grow thinner and more fragile by the day."

Margaret says, "I completely understand and know what that's like."

Sally continues, "We both took turns reading to Harrietta. Sometimes the Bible, and sometimes those romance novels she loved so very much. He refused to stop believing she'd get better. She died in his arms, Margaret. Fills me with love and a deep ache in my heart for them. Harrietta was soft spoken, warm-hearted, and a very serious woman. She had a very one-way thing about her. She was always the same, never changing. She wore the same style of clothes, never dyed her hair, wore the same haircut for as long as I had known her. She was always graceful. She had a very gentle soul. Her voice always came out in more of a whisper, even when we went to school together. She was as shy then as the last day I saw her. Very strict on herself with a routine she grew up in. She was always timely. I sure miss her." Sally finishes sorting through the streamers and balloons.

Jack walks over, "Don't worry about the balloons. We have hired a company to come in and fill this entire ceiling with them. I told them not to send me any. I wasn't interested in them, but they put some in for free, as a thank you for doing business with them."

Sally laughs and says, "Shucks, I was hoping Margaret would blow them all up!"

Margaret smiles and stands taller, "I could, too!" She straightens herself, mocking the insincerity of the matter.

"The guys will hang the streamers, but they will need to know where you ladies want them and how." Jack looks over to Sally, "Are you coming to the party?"

Sally says, "Andy and I broke up."

Jack's eyes become as huge as a wolf's that had waited for Little Red Riding Hood's entrance.

"It's about time," he says excitedly. "He was way too young to appreciate a woman like you."

Sally looks to the floor and responds, "I'm not sure how to take that."

Jack takes his finger, lifting Sally's chin, "Be my date for the New Year's Eve Party, and you'll know exactly how to take it."

Margaret feels very awkward with the intensity in Jack's eyes. She starts walking clear across to the other side of the room, taking some streamers with her. She gets to her halfway point and ends up so rushed she drops them.

Roger walks over and picks them up for her. "Glad I could be of help this time." Then he mutters, "Clumsy."

Margaret's eyebrows go up in surprise, "Did you just call me clumsy, Roger?!"

"You caught me," he laughs.

"Well I never!" Margaret laughs with him.

CHAPTER 16

Roger stares at his typewriter. He decides this time he's going to make a bold move. After working all week with Margaret, hearing his grandkids speak continuously about her at Christmas Eve dinner, and being home alone on Christmas night, he decided to put a letter under a rock of the cement bench he saw Margaret sitting at. He had peeked glances toward where she read her book. This letter would be titled to her.

Dear Margaret,
Xxx

He pulls the paper out of the typewriter, deciding it is titled too interpersonal.
He starts again.

Margaret,

This may seem silly, or maybe even fear of rejection face to face. I'm not asking for a date. I'm too old, and still in love with my wife.
Xxx

He pulls it out of the typewriter frustrated with himself, crinkling it up, and trying to aim it toward the bin next to the fireplace.

He types again.

Margaret,

Will you, I mean, do you want to go the New Year's Eve party with me? My kids tell me I need to get out more. Don't worry, it's not a date. I'm too old to date. I was thinking two friends who enjoy each other's company. I mean, maybe that is a date? Apparently, I'm not very good at this. Do you want to? to go with me? Sorry this is coming out so wrong. I guess we are imperfect. Perfectly imperfect? Laughs to you. Oh, and Merry Christmas!

CHAPTER 17

Margaret and Sally were busy all Christmas morning, throughout the day, and even late into the evening. They were serving free drinks to go with the funds donated by the community, to put toward a free buffet.

Sally says, "Thank you so much for helping me, Margaret."

Margaret replies, "Sally, lucky for me, they come to the counter to get their drinks. My feet would have never handled walking all about your café for this long." Margaret takes off her apron, while watching the last guest leave.

Margaret looks at Sally's feet and says, "I don't know how you do this every day."

"Pedicures, Marge, pedicures! Do you want to go with me next time?"

Margaret says, "Actually, there is something I want to discuss you with you, later."

Sally flips the open sign to close and says, "I'm looking forward to the New Year's Eve dance. I still can't believe Jack asked me, but I definitely need both a manicure and a pedicure."

"Then you weren't looking into his eyes, and seeing the way he was looking at you." Margaret covers her smile and snickers. "Speaking of the party, Sally, do you have a typewriter here?"

"Why? What's up?" Sally asks, as she wipes down the counter.

"I received a letter from Roger this morning. I'd like to write him back. I never learned to type. Is it like playing the piano? Now that, I can do!" Margaret tries to save herself some grace.

Sally dries her hand and says, "I have a laptop and a printer. I can type it for you. Come to the back with me."

Sally eagerly asks, "Are you going to go to the dance???"

Sally walks through the kitchen to another door, when she unlocks it she holds the door open for Margaret.

"Very nice, you are quite the decorator, Sally Marshall!" Margaret looks around, as she follows Sally to the desk.

"It's small, so I made it quaint. I wanted to walk in, take a load off, and relax. No getting past the question, Margaret. Are you going to the dance and will you be taking Roger?"

"I feel nervous. Lex never took me dancing, and what if he wants to dance??!! I don't know the first thing about it, and I'm too old. If I fall, my body will be like Humpty Dumpty, except it won't be put back together again."

Sally laughs again, "Now who is being hard on herself?!"

Sally types everything Margaret has decided to say, four different times. She says, "Uh, Margaret, my backspace finger is getting sore."

"Okay, just use the last one," Margaret says.

"I can't get it back now. Oh wait, I might be able to... let me find the undo. It is here somewhere. Oh, here it is!"

Roger,

Yes, I accept your invitation. In return, you will owe me, one game night with Eloise and Harry.
 Merry Christmas,
 Margaret

Sally says, "So cute!"

Margaret asks, "Does it sound too demanding or childish?"

"No, it sounds like a wonderful start to an enduring friendship." Sally puts it in an envelope and uses the zip lock bag Roger had put Margaret's letter in. "Come on, I will walk over with you. It's dark out now. Let's be childish and tape it to his door after ringing his bell."

Margaret explains, "Sally, I'm much too old to run. He'll see us,"

Sally says, "I will tape it to his door, and we will hide together. Then I'll walk you home."

Margaret reluctantly says, "Okay, I'm in."

CHAPTER 18

Margaret couldn't believe how many people were there. It was as if the whole suburb showed up. Most of which she had known through her years of living within the community. Roger was by her side the entire night. She hadn't laughed so much since before her Lexter was diagnosed with terminal cancer.

Margaret even danced with Roger. He moves slow enough that he makes it easy for her to follow his lead. Too soon, the band starts playing faster music and announces line dancing. Margaret quickly unfolds her arms from Roger's shoulders.

Roger releases Margaret's waist.

"Thanks for the dance, Roger. You're very good." Margaret follows Roger back to the table.

Roger replies, "I'm glad I finally talked you in to it. You're not too shabby yourself."

Jack and Sally walk over and try to convince them into doing the line dances with them.

Sally says, "Come on, Marge! I can show you how."

Margaret says, "No way. I think I pushed myself more than my body can tolerate." She smiles at Sally.

Roger and Margaret sit. They start laughing together again, as they watch Jack and Sally boot and scoot all over the dance floor, being their usual fun, loving selves.

Margaret tells Roger, "I think they go well together."

Roger said, "They certainly do, Margaret."

Soon, the night begins to reach the midnight hour as everyone begins to count down together, "10, 9, 8, 7, 6, 5, 4, 3, 2... and it is midnight folks!"

Roger holds up his glass and says, "To love that never ends, even as other love begins."

Margaret clinks her glass against his and repeats some of Roger's earlier expression, and says, "Cheers, to the imperfect kind of perfect."

Roger gives Margaret a kiss on the cheek, and says "Happy New Year's, Margaret."

Jack walks up to the band's microphone and thanks everyone for coming. He says, "It has been requested that we have one last song this midnight hour, "Auld Lang Syne." Jack takes Sally's hand and leads her to the dance floor as the band plays.

Roger reaches out his hand, and asks, "Would you like to dance with me again, Margaret?"

Margaret places her hand in his as he enfolds his fingers over hers. They dance under the disco ball, and the rest of the room fades away as they talk and stare in to each other's eyes learning more about each other with every passing moment.

Auld Lang Syne, Robert Burns

Should auld acquaintance be forgot,
And never brought to mind?
Should auld acquaintance be forgot,
And auld lang syne?

CHORUS
For auld lang syne, my jo,
For auld lang syne,
We'll tak' a cup o' kindness yet,
For auld lang syne.

And surely ye'll be your pint-stoup!
And surely I'll be mine!
And we'll tak' a cup o' kindness yet,
For auld lang syne.

CHORUS
We twa hae run about the braes,
And pou'd the gowans fine;
But we've wander'd mony a weary fit,
Sin' auld lang syne.

CHORUS
We twa hae paidl'd in the burn,
Frae morning sun till dine;
But seas between us braid hae roar'd
Sin' auld lang syne.

CHORUS
And there's a hand, my trusty fiere!
And gie's a hand o' thine!
And we'll tak' a right gude-willie waught,
For auld lang syne.

Printed in the United States
By Bookmasters